The Secret Life of
OCEANS

happy yak

Brimming with creative inspiration, how-to projects, and useful information to enrich your everyday life, quarto.com is a favorite destination for those pursuing their interests and passions.

Senior Designer: Sarah Chapman-Suire
Commissioning Editor: Carly Madden
Assistant Editor: Alice Hobbs
Creative Director: Malena Stojić
Associate Publisher: Rhiannon Findlay

First published in 2023 by Happy Yak,
an imprint of The Quarto Group.
1 Triptych Place, London
SE1 9SH, United Kingdom.
T (0)20 7700 6700 F (0)20 7700 8066
www.quarto.com

A catalogue record for this book is available from the British Library.

ISBN 978 0 7112 7869 1
eISBN 978 0 7112 7871 4

Manufactured in Guangdong, China TT012023
9 8 7 6 5 4 3 2 1

MIX
Paper from
responsible sources
FSC® C016973
www.fsc.org

CONTENTS

Hello! I'm Tia the green turtle.
I'm famous for my beautiful shell
and my swimming skills as well.
I'll share some secrets of the sea.
Would you like to explore with me?

Dear Reader,

We green turtles swim in most of the oceans of the world and we see lots of amazing sights. Let's take a swim together and I'll take you to visit some of these beautiful places. Coral reefs, seaweed forests and golden beaches will all be stop-offs on our way. As we go, we'll learn lots of incredible things and meet all sorts of animals, too.

On my underwater journeys I've heard many magical ocean stories from across the planet. I'll tell you some of them as we swim. Get ready for friendly giants, fearsome sea gods and singing mermaids.

Oh, and as we travel, look out for some special sea friends that you can spot too.

Are you ready to dive into our journey? Let's go!

Love from
Tia the green turtle

**Can you spot
Sammy the seahorse?**

He wanted to be the one to play
hide-and-seek right at the
beginning of our trip!

WHEN I WAS BORN
My dangerous dash

I was born on a beach one moonlit night...

My mum swam back to the beach where she had been born thirty years before. Later I'll tell you her secrets for finding her way back (p24).

She used her flippers to dig a deep hole in the sand. Then she laid 100 white eggs, each one the size of a ping-pong ball.

She covered us up with more sand and left for the ocean. Her job was done.

It was warm and safe in our hole. We grew in our eggs until we were ready to hatch.

We all hatched together and scrambled, higgledy-piggledy, out of the hole. We were just 5 cm long – about the size of a grown-up human's little finger.

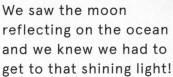

We saw the moon reflecting on the ocean and we knew we had to get to that shining light!

We scrabbled across the sand, but hungry birds were there trying to grab some of us.

I did my best. Scribble-scrabble... Was that the shadow of a bird above me?

Swish.

At last I reached the waves and I was washed from the shore. Now I was an ocean baby.

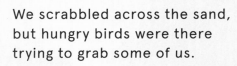

One day I will go back and lay eggs myself, but for now I am busy feeding and growing.

Can you spot a tiny hermit crab?

She's carrying her shell around. She lives inside it.

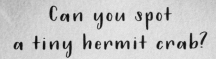

ALL ABOUT ME
Some sea turtle secrets

I am a type of animal called a **marine reptile**.

I have a great sense of smell.

I'm good at seeing underwater but I struggle to see far-away things clearly on land.

My **ears** are two hidden holes.

I use my **front flippers** to paddle.

My **head** and flippers are fixed outside my shell.

I can swim at 35km/hr – as fast as a car – if I need to escape danger.

I need to come up to the sea surface to breathe air.

My **shell** protects me from harm.

I use my **back flippers** to steer.

Yum, yum! Seagrass!
I like to eat seagrass and algae. I tear it up with my beak, which has a jagged edge for cutting. My other turtle friends prefer to hunt animals such as jellyfish. Let's meet them.

My six sea turtle friends

Kemp's Ridley
0.6 m long
(slightly bigger than the seat of a chair)

Olive Ridley
0.7 m long

Hawksbill
0.9 m long
(about the length of a shopping trolley)

Flatback
0.97 m long

Loggerhead
1 m long

Leatherback
1.8 m long
(roughly the height of an average adult)

Dive!

I'm good at diving, but leatherbacks are the champion turtle divers. They can reach over 1000 m deep (the tallest building in the world would easily sit underwater in an ocean that deep).

OUR OCEAN KINGDOMS
Five watery realms

There are five oceans on our planet. They are like five different watery kingdoms that join up with each other. I haven't visited all of them, but I have heard about them from my sea friends. Look out for some ocean creatures to spot on the map.

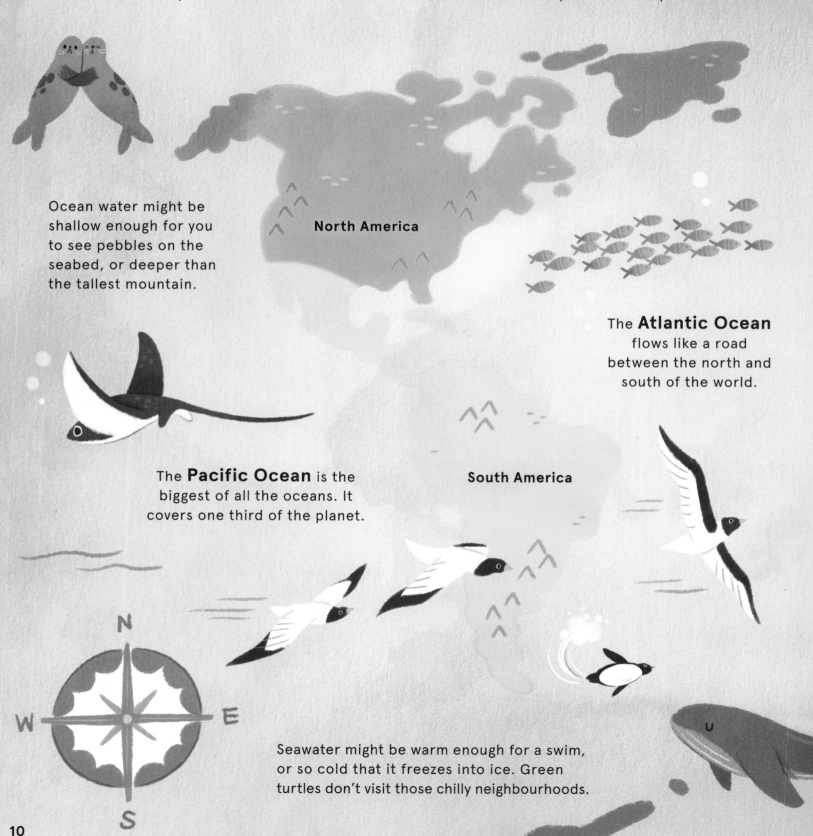

Ocean water might be shallow enough for you to see pebbles on the seabed, or deeper than the tallest mountain.

North America

The **Atlantic Ocean** flows like a road between the north and south of the world.

The **Pacific Ocean** is the biggest of all the oceans. It covers one third of the planet.

South America

Seawater might be warm enough for a swim, or so cold that it freezes into ice. Green turtles don't visit those chilly neighbourhoods.

The **Arctic Ocean** flows around the chilly north. Brrrrrr!

Our Earth is actually round like a ball but this map shows it as if it was flattened out like a piece of paper.

Europe

Asia

Africa

The **Indian Ocean** is shaped like a giant letter M.

Oceania

The **Southern Ocean** flows around the icy south. It's too cold for turtles like me.

Can you spot:

A penguin?

A killer whale?

Two seals?

Three seabirds?

An octopus?

Two shoals of fish?

Antarctica

ANGANGALO AND THE SALTY SEA

A sea tale from the Philippines

Lots of magical tales come from the shores of the Pacific Ocean. This legend comes from the Philippines, a country with thousands of islands. It's about one of the island giants and some very angry ants...

Long ago the Pacific Ocean wasn't salty, or so says this sea tale. In those far-away days, a group of island villagers used to set sail every morning for another island where they could gather salt. The villagers sold it at the market and made enough money to buy food and live well.

Angangalo was a friendly giant who lived in the mountains nearby. He was so tall that when he paddled in the Pacific Ocean, the water only came up to his knees.

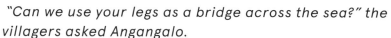

"Can we use your legs as a bridge across the sea?" the villagers asked Angangalo.
"Of course!" he boomed. He sat down and stretched his legs across the sea to the salty island. As the villagers were crossing his legs, Angangalo accidentally stuck his feet into an anthill and angry red ants began to crawl up his ankles.
Tickle, bite! Tickle, bite!
Poor Angangalo gritted his teeth and tried not to think about those angry ants until all the villagers had crossed safely.

12

Soon everybody was ready to return home with their sacks full of salt. The villagers climbed up on to Angangalo's legs, but so did the ants!

"Oh no! Hurry," Angangalo cried.

"He's afraid of tiny insects," the villagers giggled. They took no notice and they walked across slowly because their sacks were heavy.

Tickle, bite! Tickle, bite, went the angry ants.

"Gaaaaargh!" roared Angangalo. He couldn't stand it any longer and he dropped his legs into the water.

The sacks of salt splashed down into the waves and the villagers would have fallen in too if Angangalo hadn't scooped them all up and saved them.

"Sorry about that," he sighed. "It was just too tickly! Just too bitey!"

Everybody watched the salt swirling into the sea, making the seawater salty to this very day!

Seawater is always salty and that isn't really Angangalo's fault. It's because salt has been washed into it over time from the rocks and the soil on the land. I love this story though. Tickle, bite! Tickle, bite!

Can you spot two dolphins watching Angangalo?

WHO LIVES WHERE?

The depths of the ocean

The ocean is rather like an apartment block with different sea animals living on each level. Some of us like the sparkly sunshine at the surface and some of us don't mind living deep down in the dark. I'll take you on a tour to see who lives at the different levels.

The Sunlight Zone
Down to 200 m

In the top part of the ocean, sunlight shines into the water. This is where I swim, along with lots of animals you will recognize.

The Twilight Zone
Down to 1000 m

The animals who live here don't mind it being a bit gloomy. Many of them travel up to the top layer to feed at night, then swim back down here for safety in the daytime.

The Midnight Zone
Down to 4000 m

It's as dark as night here all the time, but some of the animals who live here can make their own light. They have body parts containing chemicals or bacteria that glow. It's called bioluminescence (by-oh-loom-in-es-sents). They hope the light might fool a tasty creature into coming too close and then... Gulp!

The Abyss *(ab-is)*
Down to 6000 m

Creatures who live here must be able to live in darkness and survive the heavy weight of all the water pressing down on them from above.

This is
the zone where
you would be if
you were paddling
or swimming in
the sea.

You'd need a
submarine to
visit this zone.

It's very cold
down here.
I wouldn't like it!

Hardly any humans
have ever been here.
To visit you would need a
specially built super-
tough submarine.

Can you spot
a boat bobbing on
the waves?

15

MY GIANT FRIENDS
Now THAT'S big!

Some of the ocean animals I know are unbelievably big, but don't worry! They may be giants but they aren't known to harm humans.

Blue whales are the largest creatures on Earth. They can grow as long as three coaches parked in a line and weigh as much as 30 big African elephants. They have the world's biggest babies, and they can make a noise louder than a jet plane!

24–30 m long

Blue whales eat tiny creatures called krill.

Found in every ocean except the Arctic

Whale sharks are the largest fish in the sea. They can grow as long as a school bus, but they're not scary sharks. Whale sharks swim along with their giant mouths open, gathering tiny creatures floating in the water.

5.5 m to 10 m long

Every whale shark has a different pattern of spots.

Found in warm oceans

Mouth 1.5 m wide (nearly as wide as a car)

Giant squid can grow to the size of two ice cream vans in a row. Their eyes are the size of frisbees, to help them see in the gloomy depths. Sperm whales hunt giant squid and sometimes the two will have fierce underwater battles!

12–13 m long to the tentacle tips

8 tentacles lined with powerful suckers

Found deep in oceans around the world

The **giant Pacific octopus** is usually reddish-brown, but it can quickly change colour to hide from its shark enemies. It's a hunter, too. It grabs small animals with its long tentacles, then crushes them with its tough beak.

9.8 m wide to the tips of the tentacles

8 tentacles lined with suckers

Found mostly in the North Pacific

Oarfish look like long silvery snakes and they can grow as long as four doors laid end to end! Oarfish live deep down in the ocean and they have big eyes to help them see in the dark. They gobble up small creatures that swim past.

Up to 8 m long

Oarfish live across the world but not in the coldest seas.

Ocean sunfish grow as round and wide as a garden trampoline. They live in warm oceans and sometimes like to lie at the surface, basking in the sunshine. Ocean sunfish look quite strange because they have no tail fins.

Up to 3.3 m long

Ocean sunfish eat jellyfish and small sea creatures.

Can you spot an ancient pot?

It was left behind from a shipwreck long ago.

MY TINY FRIENDS
Frilly, wiggly, feathery and curly

Now we've met the giants, let's go for a paddle to
spot some of the smallest creatures in the sea.

Billions of tiny animals are floating in the ocean waters
of the world. They're called zooplankton and some of
them are so small that humans can only see them under a
microscope. There are mini floating plant-like living things,
too, called phytoplankton (fy-toe-plank-tun).

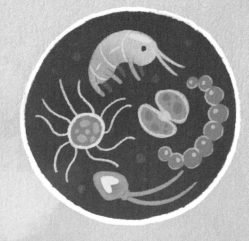

**Zooplankton and phytoplankton
are lots of different shapes.**

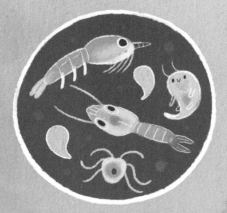

**Some of the zooplankton are
baby animals such as crabs,
lobsters and fish.**

Seahorses are tiny fish with curly
tails and long snouts that they use
to vacuum up food. There are lots
of different kinds. The tiniest one
is called the pygmy seahorse, and
it is just 16mm long – about the size
of a grown-up human's thumbnail.

**Seahorses live in sheltered spots
amongst seagrasses and seaweed.
They live amongst coral, too.**

It's tough for tiny creatures to make it in the ocean. Look at us baby green turtles. While we are growing we do our best to find food and not get gobbled up, but only one turtle in 1000 will survive and become an adult. I was very lucky!

Be careful, little turtle!

Krill swim up to the surface in the daytime and sink down deeper at night.

Krill are some of the most important mini animals in the sea. They look like see-through red prawns and grow up to 6 cm long. They live in huge shoals and lots of animals feed on them. A blue whale needs to eat 4 tonnes of krill every day. That's roughly the weight of a family car!

Imagine a tiny octopus just 2.5 cm long – about the length of a juicy green grape. That's the size of the octopus wolfi, the world's smallest octopus.

The octopus wolfi is found in the Pacific Ocean.

Can you spot a lobster trying to hide?

19

THE DAY THE SEAHORSES CAME

A sea tale from Chukotka

A cruel wave and a lucky escape

Seahorses look like tiny magical creatures, don't they? No wonder there are lots of old legends and tales about them. Here's one a seabird told me, based on an old story from chilly Siberia in the far north of the world.

Long, long ago there was a family who lived down by the sea. The grandfather of the family was a woodcarver. He was especially good at carving small figures of horses and he kept a couple in his pocket because he felt they brought him good luck. He turned out to be right!

The family often collected driftwood from the shore. After one especially big storm the grandfather and his grandson went down to the beach to collect the wood that had been washed up. A little seagull hopped after them, and they were just making friends with it when one of the waves rose magically up from the sea!

"You're coming with me to work for the King of the Sea!" it cried and it grabbed the grandson.

The family paced the beach, calling and calling. Then the little seagull swooped down and perched on the grandfather's shoulder and whispered in his ear.
"Don't worry. You'll get him back," cried the seagull.
"Dive into the sea and I promise you'll be safe. Your horses will help you."

Grandfather was amazed to find that he was able to breathe underwater. He walked along the seabed until he came to a grand palace and entered a hall made of shells. Inside sat the King of the Sea, with a shaggy beard and a seaweed coat.
"I have come for my grandson. He belongs with his family," explained the grandfather.
"But I need more servants around here. That's why I sent the wave," snapped the grumpy King.

Then the grandfather remembered the little carved horses in his pocket.
"Take these," he suggested. The instant he took the carvings out they turned into beautiful seahorses, fluttering their tiny frilly fins. The King had never seen such a thing. He was amazed!
"You may have your grandson back in return for these wonderful creatures," he declared.
The child ran to his grandfather's side and in an instant they found themselves back safely in their home by the sea.

Some say the King now gallops through the ocean in a chariot drawn by the seahorses. He loves them living in the sea and so do we!

Can you spot an anchor from an old ship down on the seabed?

HELLO! IT'S ME!
Rumbles, clicks and sea songs

Ocean animals don't talk in the same way as humans. We have other clever ways of contacting each other, using sounds that travel through the water. Here are some of our signalling secrets.

Whales or dolphins usually travel in groups called pods. They signal to each other with clicks, whistles and squawks.

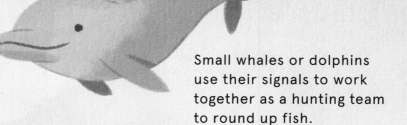

Small whales or dolphins use their signals to work together as a hunting team to round up fish.

Pods have their own special signals, just like humans have different languages. The animals in a pod can tell from the sounds other animals make who is a friend and who is a stranger.

Bottlenose dolphins each have their own unique whistle sound, which they use to say "hello" to other dolphins. It's rather like having a name.

The biggest whales often swim alone but they can signal to each other over very long distances. Blue whales make low rumbling sounds that can travel 3200 km or more through the water.

We green turtles sometimes make very low rumbling sounds to each other, too, but you wouldn't hear it. In fact, most ocean animal sounds are too low or high for humans to hear without special equipment.

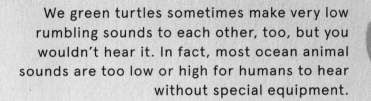

Male humpback whales are famous for their complicated singing signals. They use the singing to contact other humpback whales swimming in the ocean nearby.

Fish signal to each other with movements and sometimes even light flashes. Reef fish such as the bigeye even make croaking, purring and popping sounds. The noises probably help them stay close to each other and avoid danger.

Can you spot a jellyfish sneaking by?

23

INCREDIBLE JOURNEYS
A superpower under the sea

All of us sea turtles are brilliant at finding our way across the oceans.
One day I will travel all the way back to the beach where I was born.
How? By using my super-sense!

We all have senses that help us to understand the world around us. Touch, taste, sight, smell and hearing are a human's five senses, for example. Some of us animals have an extra skill, though. We can also sense the Earth's magnetic field.

The Earth's magnetic field is an invisible layer of magnetism around the planet. If you're not sure what magnetism is, find a magnet to play with. You'll see it can pull or push metal away with its invisible power.

The magnetic field is like an invisible map that shows me the way.

NORTH

WEST

EAST

SOUTH

My super-sense gives me a kind of magnetic map. I can find north, south, east and west wherever I am. I can also sense tiny changes in the magnetic field – rather like you might see a hill or a valley on a walk in the countryside.

I can remember the position of my home beach on the magnetic map. I can also remember things such as how it looks and smells. It's all stored in my brain like a computer file!

24

Salmon use magnetism, too. They are born in rivers far from the sea and once they're fully grown, they swim down to the ocean. Years later, when it's time for them to lay eggs, they return to the exact same spot where they were born. They swim home using their magnetic map, and they will even leap up waterfalls and over rocks to get there. They use their sense of smell, too.

Nobody knows for sure how we animals have this super-sense. It might be partly because we have tiny crystals of a magnetic material called magnetite inside our bodies. Lobsters, birds and some types of fish have it too, along with land animals such as dogs and foxes. You humans might even have some in your brain, too!

THE HUNGRY SEA TURTLE

A sea tale from Africa and the Caribbean

A greedy spider and a sea turtle

I heard this story one day when I was swimming in a lovely warm sea in the Caribbean. It's about a legendary spider called Anansi. He's in lots of stories from Africa and the Caribbean and he's always playing tricks! One day he tried fooling his old friend Sea Turtle.

Anansi was a greedy spider. When he found some really juicy yams, he cooked them all for himself.

Knock, knock.
  "Bother," thought Anansi. He opened the door to find his friend Sea Turtle.
  "Hello, Anansi. Those yams smell great. I've been on a long journey and I'm really tired and hungry. Could I come in and share your food?"

Anansi was being a meanie and he did not want to share his yams. He waited for his friend to sit down at the table and then he said:
  "Manners are very important, Sea Turtle. Your flippers are sandy and you need to wash them in the sea before you touch the food."

Sea Turtle was embarrassed that he'd forgotten his manners, so he went off to wash. Meanwhile Anansi tucked into the yams.
  "Your flippers are still dirty. You need to go back and wash them," said Anansi when Sea Turtle returned. He'd walked back up the beach and his flippers were sandy again.

This time Sea Turtle was more careful. He washed and came back across the rocks, but when he returned Anansi had eaten all the yams except for one tiny piece.
  "That's your share," he declared.
  Sea Turtle knew Anansi needed to learn a lesson.
  "Come to my house for a picnic tomorrow. I owe you, Anansi."

The next day Anansi went down to the ocean and dived in. He could see a delicious picnic laid out on the seafloor below, but there was a problem. He couldn't reach it! He didn't weigh enough to sink down, so he had to watch as Sea Turtle began nibbling the tastiest treats.

Then Anansi had an idea. He swam back to the beach and filled his coat pockets with rocks so that he was heavy enough to sink down to the seabed.
 "Welcome, Anansi. Manners are very important. I hope you agree," sighed Sea Turtle. "It would only be polite to take off your coat."

Anansi was embarrassed that he'd forgotten his manners, so he took his coat off... And guess what? He floated straight back up to the surface.
 "I think you have learned a lesson, Anansi," Sea Turtle called.
 "If you are unkind then the chances are that someone will be unkind back to you. Next time let's share our food, my friend."
 What a smart sea turtle, and what a good lesson for Anansi that day!

Can you spot a tiny crab hoping to share some of the picnic with Sea Turtle?

ADVENTURES IN THE OCEAN'S GARDENS
Tiny creatures and giant plants

Let's explore two magical places to be found in the ocean not far from the land. One is a coral reef that grows in a shallow warm sea, filled with sunlight. The other is a kelp forest that grows on underwater rocks. I like visiting them both.

Corals shaped like cabbages, fans and fingers

Corals grow in all sorts of shapes and colours. They can be hard and stony or soft like a plant.

Butterfly fish

Sea sponge

Anemone

Seaweed as tall as towering trees

Kelp is a type of thick brown seaweed that can grow up to 45 m high, about as tall as a 15-storey apartment block.

Rockfish

Compass jellyfish

Harbour seal

Sea urchin

Corals are actually tiny creatures. Some of them build stony cups at their bases. Their tiny tentacles pop out above the cup, to catch food from the water.

Tentacles

Stony cup

Reef

When a stony coral dies, it leaves its cup behind. More corals grow on top, and over thousands of years a whole reef builds up.

Clownfish

Parrotfish

Sea otters live among the kelp forests in the eastern Pacific. They eat the sea urchins that munch on the kelp.

Sea otter

Ruby octopus

A sea otter will find a sea urchin and a stone. Then it will float on its back and bash the urchin open with the stone, using its chest as a table. Clever!

ICY WORLDS OF WONDER
Chilly, slippery, stormy spots

There are two chilly oceans around the top and bottom of the world. I don't visit them but my friends the seabirds have told me all about them. The thought of swimming there makes me shiver!

The sea of floating ice

In the far north of the world, winter is so cold that part of the Arctic Ocean freezes over. The huge raft of floating ice is called an ice pack.

Harp seal

Amphipods

Millions of tiny shrimps called amphipods live upside-down under the ice. They make a meal for bigger animals such as whales and seals.

The realm of the penguins

The Antarctic is in the far south of the world. It is a giant section of land surrounded by the super-stormy Southern Ocean. The land is icy all the time and in winter the ocean freezes over. In summer lots of animals visit to have their babies.

Adélie penguin

King penguin

All sorts of penguins breed around the Antarctic region. They waddle around on land, but they're great swimmers when they go hunting in the water for fish.

All sorts of whales visit the Arctic but the most unusual is the male narwhal. It has a long tusk like a unicorn.

Arctic skua

The biggest and fiercest Arctic animal, the **polar bear**, can swim. Polar bears hunt seals to eat.

Walrus

Arctic cod

Male narwhal

Icefish

Fish that live in such cold waters have a clever secret to help them survive. They have a special substance in their blood to stop it freezing up.

Elephant seals

Toothfish

Elephant seals visit the Antarctic region to breed. They bask on the ice or gather on the island of South Georgia in a noisy smelly crowd of around 120,000.

DANGER!
Scary teeth and secret spines

The oceans aren't peaceful places. There are lots of animals out to eat each other! There are some particularly fearsome enemies that I definitely need to avoid.

Tiger sharks will eat almost anything, including sea turtles. They get their name because the young sharks have skin stripes. They can grow as long as a family car and their sharp teeth can cut and tear. They swim in warm seas and I never want to bump into one!

The **great white shark** is the biggest hunting shark in the world and the most scary. They have 300 sharp teeth and an incredibly powerful bite that can slice through just about any living thing. Great whites live in warm and warmish waters around the world.

Baby sea turtles have a lot of enemies because they make an easy snack. Sea lions, octopuses, seals and even **meat-eating fish** would like to swallow a baby sea turtle. Let's hope those little guys can hide when they need to.

Hammerhead sharks will eat small turtle species. Their strange-looking spread-out nose gives them hunting superpowers. They can smell their prey and also sense tiny electrical signals given out by living creatures as they move. Hammerhead sharks sometimes cruise through the kelp forests. Creepy!

We turtles aren't completely defenceless. We're fast swimmers and we can also flip sideways and swim with our wide protective shell facing the enemy.

Young green turtles sometimes hunt jellyfish and we have a clever way of avoiding the stings on their long tentacles. There are protective spines lining my mouth and my throat all the way down to my stomach.

Jellyfish can give a painful sting, but not to me.

Can you spot three treasure coins?

BATTLE OF THE GUARDIANS

A sea tale from Fiji

A bully meets his match

Fiji has many islands, most of them surrounded by coral reefs.
In old legends, each island had its own sea creature god to guard it –
and sometimes the guardians fought each other like superheroes.

The most arrogant guardian of all was a shark god called Dakuwaqa.
 "I can beat anyone in a fight, so everybody should obey me. Sharks rule!" he would crow.

Dakuwaqa was a fearsome fighter with rows of gleaming teeth and a thrashing tail. He loved to challenge the other guardians to fights. During these fights, big waves would crash onto the shore. The sea was not safe for the islanders to swim in due to Dakuwaqa's fighting.

One day, Dakuwaqa heard some of the other sharks nervously muttering to each other.
 "You all sound as weak as jellyfish! What are you afraid of?" Dakuwaqa demanded.
 "It's the guardian of Kadavu. He is too strong for anyone," they explained.

 "What! Nobody is stronger than me, do you hear? Nobody!" shouted Dakuwaqa as he rushed off to Kadavu. The guardian of Kadavu was the octopus god Rokobakaniceva. His name was as mighty as he was, so we'll call him Roko for short.

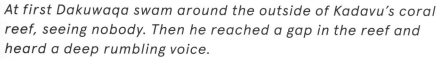

At first Dakuwaqa swam around the outside of Kadavu's coral reef, seeing nobody. Then he reached a gap in the reef and heard a deep rumbling voice.

"Nobody gets past me. Stay away from my island."
A huge octopus crawled into view. Four of his arms were securely anchored to the reef and the other four floated free.

"We'll see about that!" cried Dakuwaqa and he shot forward with his mouth open and all his teeth showing.

Roko was not scared. In a flash Dakuwaqa found two long arms wrapped round his body. Roko's arms began to squeeze until Dakuwaqa could hardly breathe.

"Gggggfff! Igggvnnn!" he mumbled, unable to speak.
Roko loosened the tentacle round the shark.

"What was that you said?" he asked.

"Get off! I give in!" moaned Dakuwaqa.

"Hmmm. First you must promise to protect the people of my island whenever they go out in their boats," said Roko.

"I will! I promise!" squeaked Dakuwaqa.

Roko let him go and Dakuwaqa was a much humbler shark god from that day on. He realized that he wasn't the best at everything and he shouldn't bully everyone into obeying him. Dakuwaqa also kept his promise, and the people of Kadavu were never bothered by sharks again.

WONDROUS WATER
The sea, the moon and the wind

Ocean water is always moving. It can flow smoothly along, giving me a free ride, or it can smash and crash in a storm. Here are some of its secrets.

Waves are mostly caused by the wind blowing over the water. However, underwater earthquakes and volcanic eruptions can cause waves, too. The biggest waves can be as high as apartment blocks.

Strong stormy winds bring big waves that crash against rocks, reefs and beaches. The sea churns like a washing machine in shallow waters and it's time for us sea creatures to swim to deeper, calmer locations for a while.

The top of a wave is called the crest. The bottom of the wave is called the trough. The distance between two waves is called the wavelength. In stronger winds, waves get closer together and the sea gets choppier. Watch out!

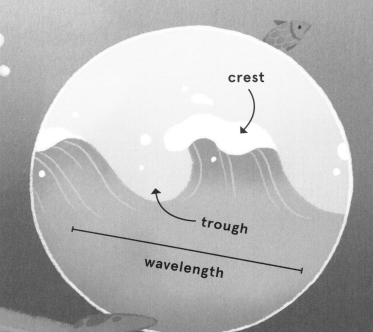

crest

trough

wavelength

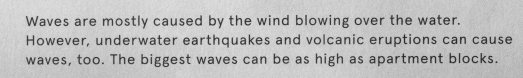

Currents around the world:

Rannell

Alaskan

Kuroshio

There are giant rivers of water that flow like pathways around the oceans. They are called currents and I use them to help carry me along on my journeys. Some are at the surface and others are deep down. Some are short and others flow right around the planet. The world's currents have different names. A few of them are shown above.

The Moon pulls the Earth's oceans towards it with a pulling force called gravity. As the Earth spins in space, different oceans begin bulging towards the Moon at different times of day. This makes water levels rise or fall in different locations. It's called high tide or low tide. If you visit a beach, you will notice the tides as the water rises up the beach or slips away.

Something unusual can also happen in the sea at the Equator, the area around the middle of the Earth. Because of the Equator's hot weather there might be no wind at all for weeks, leaving the sea flat and calm with no waves. It's an area of the oceans called the Doldrums.

Occasionally, something very strange can happen between the sea and the sky. Wind can begin to spin around and suck up a column of water like a tornado. It's called a waterspout. It doesn't usually last long, but it can do damage, so I don't want to be nearby when it happens!

Can you spot five silver fish and one red fish?

Labrador

East Australian

Canary

North Pacific

Gulf Stream

Peruvian

Florida

WHAT TO SPOT
Secrets of the coast

I sometimes see you humans when I'm near the coast. You might be in boats, swimming or perhaps walking along by the edge of the waves. Here are some shore secrets I thought you might like to look out for if you're ever down by the sea.

Coastlines don't all look the same. Some might have beaches and others might have cliffs. As the sea pounds against the shore, it creates different shapes and landscapes.

Sometimes the water wears away an arch shape.

Seawater hollows out rock cracks to make caves.

If an arch collapses, it might leave a pillar of rock called a stack.

The ocean waves slowly grind rocks into stones, then pebbles and eventually tiny particles that get dropped onto the shore to make sandy beaches.

Beaches in Bermuda have pale pink beaches made from worn-down red coral.

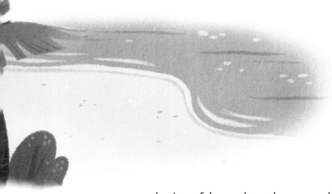

Lots of beaches have pale yellowish sand made from worn-down sandstone rock.

Some beaches in Hawaii have black sand made from volcanic lava.

There are all sorts of animals and plants to find on a beach.
Next time you visit, see how many of these you can spot.

Seaweed is often washed up on the shore. There are lots of different types. *Sea lettuce, dead man's shoelaces, sea spaghetti and landlady's wig* are all seaweeds!

Limpets are creatures that live inside shells. A limpet has a very powerful foot which clamps it to a rock. It's almost impossible to prize it off!

Tough grasses might be growing on sand dunes at the back of the beach.

Look out for empty shells washed up on the shore. Animals once lived inside them.

Lugworms burrow under the sand and make little wiggly piles above, called worm casts.

Tiny fish and crabs might be hiding in rockpools. Always keep an eye on the tide, though! Make sure you're off the beach when the sea starts to come in.

OCEAN FOLK

Living and working with the waves

Some humans live down by the seashore and even on the waves.
My wish is that we can all share the ocean peacefully together.

The Bajau People live in wooden houses on stilts off the coast of Sulawesi Island, Malaysia. The children of the Bajau often learn to swim before they can walk. Their neighbourhood is the sea and they travel through it by boat.

People who live down by the sea often have jobs to do with the ocean, too. They might have fishing boats or work in boat yards, or they might run seaside activities, cafes and hotels for visitors.

Some people choose to live full-time on an ocean-going boat, travelling between different places. If there are children onboard, they are usually homeschooled as they sail around on their ocean adventure.

Studying the oceans and ocean life is called oceanography. Scientists learning about the oceans might work onboard a ship, or they might even dive underwater in a minisub. If you love the ocean, perhaps you will study oceanography one day.

Can you spot three starfish?

THE MERMAID OF ZENNOR

A sea tale from England

A mystery singer of the sea

Stories about merpeople have been told for thousands of years around the Atlantic Ocean. The mermaid in this legend is said to have visited a tiny fishing village called Zennor, on the rocky coast of Cornwall in southwestern England.

If you are ever lucky enough to visit the Cornish village of Zennor, make sure you go into St. Senara Church to see a true treasure – a mysterious mermaid carved into a wooden bench. The carving has been in the church for around 600 years, reminding everyone of a story from long ago.

The legend began when a beautiful lady started coming to Sunday services at the church. Nobody knew who she was, only that she had a wonderful singing voice. A young man called Matthew Trewella was the best singer in the village at the time. He decided to discover who this lovely new visitor was.
"I would love to sing a song with her," he thought. So one morning after church, he followed her off towards the shore... And he never came back!

Years passed and nobody could explain Matthew's strange disappearance. Then a sea captain got a big surprise when he anchored his ship in a nearby cove. "Excuse me. Could you move your anchor?" a voice called out. The captain looked over the side of the ship and was amazed to see a mermaid in the water.

"Your anchor is blocking the doorway to my house. My husband, Matthew, and my children are inside," she explained. It was the mysterious lady that Matthew had followed. She was none other than Morveren, daughter of Llyr, the King of the Ocean!

Matthew never came back to land but he did help his friends, the fisherfolk of Zennor. Whenever the weather was going to be good, they would hear him and his mermaid wife singing softly and sweetly in the cove. When it was set to be stormy, Matthew and Morveren would warn the villagers by singing deep and low.

Perhaps Atlantic mermaid stories began because people once mistook seals for merpeople. We will never know! It is true that large parts of the world's oceans are still unexplored and there are probably plenty of real-life sea creatures still to discover.

WE NEED SAVING!
Our ocean battle

Like quite a few sea creatures, we turtles are in a struggle to survive.
We need help from you humans.

Some turtle species are in great danger of dying out altogether. The kemp's ridley and hawksbill turtles are critically endangered, which means they could soon disappear. The rest of us are dropping in numbers, too, and we all need help.

Around the world marine scientists, who study the ocean, are trying to discover as much as they can about what's happening to us. Perhaps one day you might do the same.

Our nesting sites can be damaged by careless holidaymakers or by buildings being put up nearby. If the buildings are brightly lit, baby turtles can mistake them for the moonlit sea and crawl the wrong way.

Volunteers try to keep nesting beaches safe and rescue babies who have crawled the wrong way.

Lots of sea creatures get caught up and accidentally killed in the fishing nets of trawler ships. Once a turtle gets tangled in a net it will die because it cannot get to the surface to breathe.

Nets can be fitted with excluder bars to keep out large creatures such as turtles.

Sadly, in some parts of the world turtles are illegally caught to eat and to sell. Our shells are made into souvenirs.

Tortoiseshell is banned in much of the world. Selling it is against the law.

A big danger to us is **rubbish** and **pollution** in the ocean water. We turtles can mistake a floating plastic bag for a jellyfish, swallow it and die.

Rubbish gets washed into the oceans from the land. Never drop rubbish, wherever you are.

BE A TURTLE FRIEND
Clean up and help us

You can help the oceans by doing small but important things and getting your friends and family to do the same.

BUY RIGHT
Get your family to buy fish that's marked 'sustainable'. That means it's caught in a way that's officially safer for the rest of us sea creatures. Look for the markings on tins and on menus if you eat out.

ADOPT ME!
Never buy souvenirs made of tortoiseshell or coral taken from reefs. Instead use your pocket money to adopt a turtle through a turtle-helping charity.

WORLD CLEAN-UP DAY
Every year in September volunteers around the world come out to help clean beaches, woods and town streets. You could join in!

The land and the oceans fit together
like the pieces in a jigsaw puzzle.
Take care of them as best you can -
the streams, the rivers, the oceans blue...
Try to be kind whatever you do.

Remember when you visit the beach.
Remember when you shop for fish.
Remember when you say no to plastic,
to be the best that you can be, and
remember...
remember...
remember...
me!

With Love from
Tia the turtle

To our oceans,
for all the wonders,
beauty and life
they bring us – V.M.

For Dimitris Aronis,
who lives on beautiful Paxos
and loves turtles. – M.B.